DATE DUE

GAYLORD			PRINTED IN U.S.A.

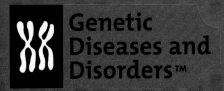

Genetic Diseases and Disorders™

Cystic Fibrosis

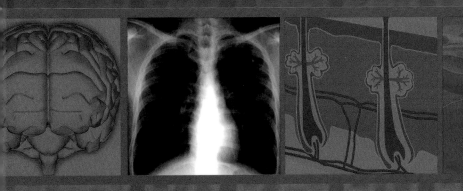

Maxine Rosaler

The Rosen Publishing Group, Inc., New York

Published in 2007 by The Rosen Publishing Group, Inc.
29 East 21st Street, New York, NY 10010

Library of Congress Cataloging-in-Publication Data

Rosaler, Maxine.
Cystic fibrosis / Maxine Rosaler.—1st ed.
    p. cm.—(Genetic diseases and disorders)
Includes bibliographical references and index.
ISBN 1-4042-0696-5 (library binding)
1. Cystic fibrosis—Juvenile literature.
I. Title. II. Series.
RC858.C95R64 2007
616.3'72—dc22

                                                      2005034811

Printed in the United States of America

On the cover: Background: A color-enhanced electron microscope image of normal, healthy lung tissue. Inset: A chest X-ray.

Contents

Introduction

Cystic fibrosis is one of the most common—and lethal—genetic diseases, afflicting 1 out of every 3,500 white children born each year in the United States and 1 in 12,000 nonwhite children. Thirty thousand children and adults in the United States suffer from cystic fibrosis. The disease, which usually makes its first appearance before a child reaches the age of three, gravely impairs the ability of its victims to breathe and digest food.

The parents of a child who has cystic fibrosis may notice that he or she has very salty skin. Other early symptoms include persistent coughing, often with a large amount of mucus, and wheezing or shortness of breath. Recurrent and chronic (repeated and frequent) infections of the airways are typical. Children with cystic fibrosis often have trouble gaining weight, and their bowel movements are excessively greasy and bulky.

As they grow older, patients with cystic fibrosis often experience frequent bouts of pneumonia and bronchitis (both are serious respiratory infections), asthma, collapsed lungs, and bleeding lungs. They also suffer from chronic diarrhea, malnourishment, diabetes, liver disease, infertility, and even lung and heart failure. Since it attacks so many body systems at once—respiratory, digestive, reproductive—cystic fibrosis is difficult for doctors to understand and even more difficult for them to treat. It remains a disease that presents the medical community with many unsolved puzzles.

Throughout human history, cystic fibrosis has often led to early death, usually in childhood. Today, better treatments are available, and people with cystic fibrosis are living longer. Indeed, some patients live long enough to have children of their own. Even so, cystic fibrosis continues to drastically shorten the lives of people afflicted with it.

It is generally agreed that the best hope for the cure of this deadly disease lies in a set of new medical techniques called gene therapy. Scientists hope to figure out how to use this revolutionary approach to fix the defective genes that cause people to develop cystic fibrosis.

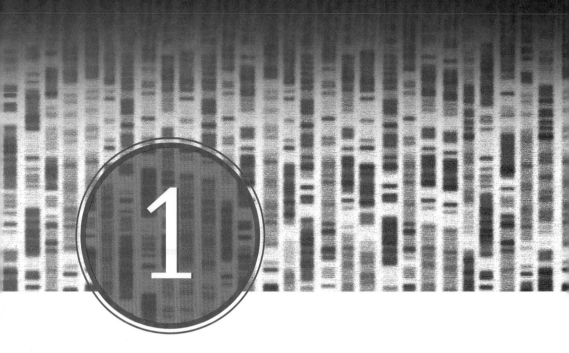

1

We call cystic fibrosis a genetic disease, but what does that mean? To begin with, it means that the disease results from a mistake in the biological process by which we inherit physical and behavioral characteristics from our parents, grandparents, and more distant ancestors. Cystic fibrosis is difficult to cure since its causes lie deep within the genetic code of its victims, pervading each of their cells.

With infectious diseases, the enemy is a germ, an alien invader that can usually be killed with drugs. With genetic diseases, the enemy is a flaw that exists within the body itself—in its genetic code—and has existed within the person's body since the moment of conception. Identifying the cause of cystic fibro-sis was difficult. Treating and curing it remains beyond the reach of modern medicine, but hopefully not for much longer.

Genes and Genetics

Because cystic fibrosis is a genetic disease, we need to know some basic genetics to understand it. All living things inherit their physical characteristics from their parents. Genes are the molecular units of information that are passed on from parent to offspring. They contain the blueprint, or plan, that determines how our bodies will develop. Characteristics ranging from the color of our eyes to our height to the tone of our voice result from the genes we have inherited from our parents, who in turn inherited genes from their parents. The same principle is true for animals and plants: the genes in a maple tree seed instruct it to grow into a maple tree— with characteristics similar to its parent's—rather than into an oak tree.

Genes are made of deoxyribonucleic acid (DNA), a long, double-stranded molecule that is shaped like a spiral staircase. The steps on the DNA staircase are chemicals that form a kind of alphabet, which scientists call the genetic code. Each strand of DNA contains thousands of genes.

Every person has two copies of every gene. One is inherited from the mother and one from the father. If a genetic trait is recessive, such as blue eye color, a person needs to inherit two copies of the gene for that trait to be expressed. Thus, brown-eyed parents both have to be carriers of the blue eye gene in order to have a blue-eyed child. Carriers of a recessive gene are heterozygous for that gene—they contain different versions of a gene on each of two corresponding chromosomes. If both parents are carriers of a recessive gene, there is a 25 percent chance that their child

CGATTCTGAACATGATACGTACTGGTCCACTAGAACTGAACTCGAGAGGTACTAGA

will show the recessive trait. That child would be homozygous for the recessive trait—he or she would have two copies of the recessive gene.

Mutations

When cell reproduction takes place, the double-stranded DNA molecule splits into two separate strands. The cell then completes each half of the original DNA molecule by filling in the missing "steps." This results in two identical copies of the original molecule. With the help of this copying process, DNA and the genetic information it contains are passed down through the generations. Usually, the copies that result are exact duplicates. However, the copies are not always perfect. A copy of a gene that has a mistake in it is called a mutated gene. The mutated gene is a little different from the original, and it does not work in exactly the same way as the original one did. In some cases, it does not work at all. Cystic fibrosis is the result of just such a genetic mutation.

Cystic Fibrosis and the Laws of Probability

It was not until 1989 that scientists first identified the gene that, when it is mutated and does not work properly, leads to cystic fibrosis. Scientists called this gene cystic fibrosis trans-membrane conductance regulator (CFTR). The gene helps regulate salt and fluid levels in cells (see chapter 2 for a more detailed description of the gene, its function, and the mutations that cause cystic fibrosis). The problem in the CFTR gene arises from an inherited mutation that disables the gene, preventing it from doing the work it is supposed to do. This mutation is recessive.

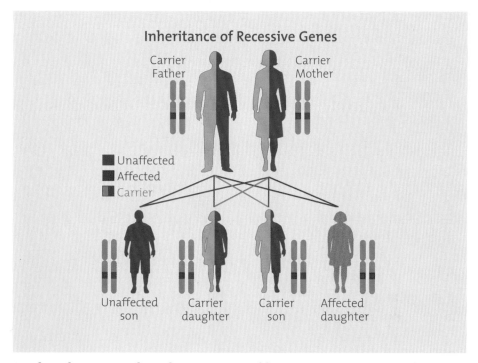

Inheritance of Recessive Genes

Carrier Father

Carrier Mother

■ Unaffected
■ Affected
■ Carrier

Unaffected son

Carrier daughter

Carrier son

Affected daughter

As the above graphic shows, cystic fibrosis occurs in people who have inherited two copies of a defective gene, one from each parent. Cystic fibrosis carriers, who have only one copy of the gene, do not have the disease, but they may pass it on to their children.

Cystic fibrosis, like other recessive genetic disorders, occurs when both parents are carriers and each contributes a defective CFTR gene to the embryo. If both parents are heterozygous for the disorder (carriers), the chance of their child inheriting two disease genes (making him or her homozygous for the disease) is 25 percent. Fifty percent of the time, the child will inherit only one disease gene from carrier parents, making him or her a carrier, too. When one of the parents is

ATCGATTCTGAACATGATACGTACTGGTCCACTAGAACTGAACTCGAGAGGTACTA

Dr. Francis Collins *(center)*, currently the director of the National Human Genome Research Institute, was the codiscoverer of the CFTR gene. Mutations on the CFTR gene interfere with its proper functioning and cause cystic fibrosis.

homozygous (and therefore actually suffering from the disease) and the other parent is a carrier, the child has a 50 percent chance of inheriting two disease genes and developing cystic fibrosis.

Five percent of people of European descent are carriers of the cystic fibrosis mutation. If two of these carriers, each of whom has a good copy of the gene and a bad copy of the gene, conceive a baby together, there is a 50 percent chance that the baby will be a carrier of the defective gene (inheriting one good gene and one bad one, like the parents). There

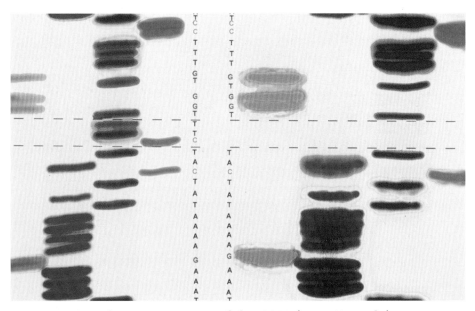

A comparison between a part of the DNA (genetic code) sequence of a healthy individual *(left)* and a part of the DNA sequence of a cystic fibrosis patient *(right)* appears above. The DNA sequences are seen as a series of colored bands. The letters running down the center denote base sequences that indicate genes that code for proteins. In both images, the protein that appears is the CFTR gene. The dotted lines running horizontally through the middle indicate the site on the CFTR gene where the cystic fibrosis mutation occurs. The lack of genetic coding at the site in the right-hand image indicates a mutated and improper functioning gene that will cause cystic fibrosis.

is a 25 percent chance that the baby will not inherit the defective gene at all, having instead one good gene from each parent. Finally, there is a 25 percent chance that the child will inherit a defective gene from each parent and therefore develop cystic fibrosis.

CGATTCTGAACATGATACGTACTGGTCCACTAGAACTGAACTCGAGAGGTACTAG

Does the CFTR Mutation Serve a Healthy Purpose?

For reasons that scientists have not yet been able to figure out completely, mutations of the CFTR gene—the mutations that lead to cystic fibrosis—are more common among northern Europeans (and people of northern European descent) than they are among other populations of people around the world. In the United States, one out of twenty-nine people of European descent carries a copy of a defective CFTR gene, while only one out of ninety Asian Americans is a carrier of a defective CFTR gene. Approximately one out of sixty-five African Americans is a carrier.

Scientists speculate that the genetic mutations that cause cystic fibrosis are more prevalent among people of northern European descent because they are of some use to these people. Carriers of the defective CFTR gene are less likely to succumb to certain types of diarrhea. Up until modern times, diarrhea was a frequent cause of death in Europe. The CFTR mutation may have protected carriers. Their children would often inherit the mutation. The consequence of this would be the presence of many copies of the mutated gene within this particular geographic population.

2

Since the CFTR gene controls a basic life process—the regulation of salt and fluids in the body—human beings have always had the CFTR gene. Genes are subject to mutation at any time, so it is difficult to pinpoint exactly when the first mutation to the CFTR gene resulting in cystic fibrosis occurred. By sampling the variations of a particular CFTR mutation in 17,000 people throughout Europe, however, geneticists have traced the defective gene to 52,000 years ago, when people from the Near East began to migrate to northern Europe. This is the earliest known appearance of that particular mutation to the CFTR gene, though mutations to the gene have probably existed since soon after the gene itself first developed.

CGATTCTGAACATGATACGTACTGGTCCACTAGAACTGAACTCGAGAGGTACTAGA

The first descriptions of people suffering from what appears to be cystic fibrosis did not appear until far later, however. A saying from the Middle Ages, preserved in a book called *German Children's Songs and Games from Switzerland,* predicts a bad end for children who have foreheads that taste salty: "Woe to that child which when kissed on the forehead tastes salty. He is bewitched and soon must die." In 1606, Alonso y de los Ruyzes de Fonteca, a Spanish professor of medicine, wrote that the fingers taste salty after rubbing the forehead of a "bewitched" child. Since excessively salty sweat is a symptom of cystic fibrosis, historians conclude that these observations refer to sufferers of that disease.

Identifying Cystic Fibrosis

Today, scientists have concluded that many patients with an unidentified disease described by doctors from the seventeenth century onward were actually suffering from cystic fibrosis. However, the disease did not receive international attention until descriptions of it were published in a report written in 1938 by Dr. Dorothy Andersen, a pathologist at Columbia-Presbyterian's Babies and Children's Hospital in New York City.

A pathologist is a doctor who specializes in the interpretation and diagnosis of the changes in tissues and body fluids caused by disease. Dr. Andersen examined the bodies and organs of infants who had died at the hospital. She noticed that a pattern of disease existed among many of the patients she studied. Wishing to understand this phenomenon, she sought out data from similar cases from colleagues at other hospitals.

Dr. Andersen reported her conclusions in a paper entitled "Cystic fibrosis of the pancreas and its relation to celiac disease." In her paper, Andersen reported that the major

In 1958, Dr. Dorothy Andersen *(center)* received an award for her pioneering identification of cystic fibrosis from Robert Natal *(right)*, president of the New York chapter of the National Cystic Fibrosis Foundation, and Victor Blitzer, the group's former president.

symptoms common to cystic fibrosis sufferers included changes in the tissues of the lungs, intestines, and pancreas. She named the disease cystic fibrosis of the pancreas because she found cysts (fluid-filled sacs) and fibers (of scar tissue) in the pancreases of the bodies she studied.

In the early 1940s, Andersen and a colleague named R. C. Hodges studied the family history of 103 children with cystic fibrosis. From their observations, they concluded that cystic

TCGATTCTGAACATGATACGTACTGGTCCACTAGAACTGAACTCGAGAGGTACTAC

fibrosis followed patterns typical of genetic diseases that are passed on by recessive genes. Two carriers—two individuals who each possess a recessive gene for a disease—can have a child together who inherits both recessive genes and, as a result, develops the disease. Andersen and Hodges pointed to many case studies that showed one child out of four in a single family having cystic fibrosis, which is the statistical pattern characteristic of families in which each parent is a carrier of a gene that causes a disease.

Determining that cystic fibrosis was a genetic disease linked to a recessive gene was an important finding, but it did not explain what caused cystic fibrosis. Understanding the cause of a disease involves more than just understanding why one person and not another contracts the disease. It means knowing what exactly has gone wrong in the body and why this particular flaw leads to the many symptoms associated with the illness. The causes, symptoms, and progression of cystic fibrosis are very complicated, so a thorough understanding and knowledge of the disease have been long in coming. Indeed, to this day, the puzzle of cystic fibrosis remains largely unsolved.

Struggling to Understand the Disease and Its Symptoms

In the years following Dorothy Andersen's identification of cystic fibrosis, physicians studying the disease focused their research on its various symptoms. Identification of the main symptom of cystic fibrosis was one of their main goals. They wanted to know which symptom indicated the main problem causing all the other symptoms.

As often happens with a complicated disease whose root cause is unknown, the theories that the scientists initially developed about cystic fibrosis tended to diverge from each other and lacked a central focus. The approach that scientists took in studying cystic fibrosis brings to mind the parable about the blind men and the elephant. As the story goes, the blind man nearest the trunk says that the elephant resembles a python. The blind man touching the body says the elephant is like a wall. The blind man touching a leg says the elephant is like a tree. Similarly, researchers were zeroing in on individual manifestations and symptoms without clearly seeing the totality of the disease.

Physicians studying cystic fibrosis were of course aware that, in order to fully understand the disease, their theories would have to account for all of its many symptoms. Nevertheless, the theories that researchers developed tended to center around whatever their medical specialty happened to be. They were confident that their particular area of expertise held the solution to the puzzle of cystic fibrosis. This narrow approach resulted in the researchers leaving several of the disease's symptoms unexplained.

In fairness, it should be pointed out that cystic fibrosis presents a bewildering array of symptoms, each of which aggravates the others. Physicians were hard pressed to identify exactly what lay at the root of all these seemingly unrelated disorders.

Patients with cystic fibrosis show evidence of having problems in four basic body systems: the respiratory system, which has the job of getting oxygen from the outside environment into the bloodstream; the gastrointestinal system, which digests food and gets rid of waste; the reproductive system, which allows humans to conceive and bear children; and the endocrine system, which includes sweat glands responsible for cooling the body and removing salt from the body.

CGATTCTGAACATGATACGTACTGGTCCACTAGAACTGAACTCGAGAGGTACTAGA

The body of a person with cystic fibrosis produces large quantities of mucus, which can block many of the body's tissues and interfere with their operation. The illustration at left shows how mucus causes blockages in the lungs, resulting in respiratory infections.

The Effects of Cystic Fibrosis on the Human Body

Respiratory System Cystic fibrosis affects the respiratory system by producing a thick, sticky mucus that blocks breathing passages. Chronic (frequent and repeated) swelling and irritation of the lining of the airways can result in asthma. In addition to interfering with breathing, the mucus makes it difficult for the body to get rid of bacteria and viruses in the airways. Often the result is chronic infections—such as pneumonia, bronchitis, and bronchiectasis—and inflammation that can cause serious, long-term lung damage. This can include lung bleeding, lung collapse, and respiratory and heart failure.

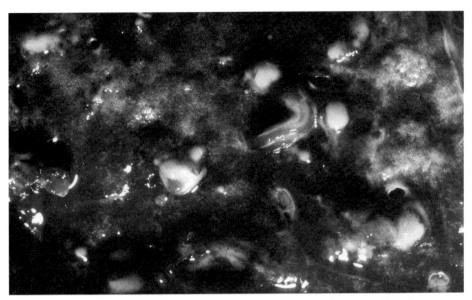

Mucus plugs the dilated bronchi (swollen lung tissue) of a twenty-year-old man in the above close-up photograph. Excessive mucus in the lungs makes breathing a struggle for many cystic fibrosis patients.

Gastrointestinal System Another set of cystic fibrosis symptoms harms the gastrointestinal system—the body system that digests food, absorbs nutrients, and produces waste, which is removed from the body. Cystic fibrosis causes a blockage in the pancreas, a gland that plays a crucial role in digestion. This prevents important pancreatic enzymes from being released. Enzymes are chemicals that speed up chemical reactions. They are used to digest food. There are different enzymes to digest fats, proteins, and carbohydrates. When there is a deficiency of these pancreatic enzymes, the digestive system has a much harder time digesting food and extracting nutrients from it. Cystic fibrosis patients often

TCGATTCTGAACATGATACGTACTGGTCCACTAGAACTGAACTCGAGAGGTACTAG

have unusually large appetites yet still suffer from malnutrition. Inadequate nutrition leads to stunted growth, poor
development of organs, and other symptoms related to vitamin deficiencies. It also makes it harder for cystic fibrosis
patients to gain the physical strength and efficient immune
system responses necessary to deal with the other challenges
presented by the disease. Some cystic fibrosis patients will
also develop diabetes because a blocked pancreas cannot
properly control the levels of sugar in the blood.

Reproductive System Cystic fibrosis has many effects on the
reproductive systems of men and women who suffer from
the disease. In both men and women, sexual development
may be delayed. In men, the thick fluids typical of the disease block the tube that connects the testicles (where sperm
is produced) and the prostate gland (where the semen that
suspends and carries the sperm is produced). As a result,
most men with cystic fibrosis are infertile (unable to produce children). However, new fertility treatments and
surgical procedures are allowing some men with cystic
fibrosis to father children. Although cystic fibrosis does not
make women infertile, the abnormal amounts of mucus and
electrolytes (ionized molecules including salt and potassium)
present in their uteruses make it difficult for them to conceive. Their general poor health, especially their poor lung
function, can also make it difficult to carry a baby to term
and make the pregnancy and birth dangerous for them.

Sweat Glands One of the most reliable indicators of cystic fibrosis is the loss of excessive amounts of salt in the
patients' sweat. This means the sufferers do not have
enough salt available for the many bodily processes that
depend on that important electrolyte, including proper
nerve and muscle function.

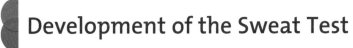

Development of the Sweat Test

In 1948, a heat wave in New York City caused the deaths of a dozen or more babies with cystic fibrosis. Dr. Paul di Sant'Agnese, a physician at the city's Babies and Children's Hospital, wondered why cystic fibrosis sufferers should be particularly susceptible to heat prostration (exhaustion or collapse). Could it be that babies with cystic fibrosis were losing too much salt through sweat? Chloride and sodium, the elements in salt, were both observed in unusually high concentrations in the sweat of patients with cystic fibrosis. Dr. di Sant'Agnese reviewed historical medical records, studied folklore that included many references to "bewitched" children with salty sweat, and made his own direct observations of patients. In 1953, he delivered a paper to the American Pediatrics Society that suggested that salt loss was one of the most important and dangerous symptoms of cystic fibrosis.

Salt is crucial to the proper functioning of the body. In addition to being necessary for healthy nervous system performance, it is also responsible for regulating many chemical reactions in the body and maintaining a proper balance among the body's fluids.

Thanks to di Sant'Agnese's pioneering observations, the measurement of salt concentration in patients' sweat became a reliable tool for diagnosing cystic fibrosis. In 1953, a relatively painless way of inducing sweat for what was called the sweat test was developed by Dr. di Sant'Agnese and a colleague. The sweat test became the most reliable method for diagnosing cystic fibrosis until 1989, when the gene whose malfunction causes cystic fibrosis was first identified.

Although the unusual amount of salt that is secreted by the sweat glands of patients with cystic fibrosis proved to be useful in diagnosing the disease, scientists also found this

TCGATTCTGAACATGATACGTACTGGTCCACTAGAACTGAACTCGAGAGGTACTAC

Dr. Paul di Sant'Agnese, shown here in his lab, developed the sweat test for cystic fibrosis in 1953. He was also one of the founders of the Cystic Fibrosis Foundation and helped to improve treatment of the disease in the United States.

particular symptom to be puzzling because it did not support earlier theories that cystic fibrosis is basically "a state of thickened mucus." There was no apparent connection between the theory of thickened mucus and di Sant'Agnese's findings about salt in the sweat. The sweat glands of cystic fibrosis patients do not contain an excess of mucus. Once again, an accurate diagnosis and complete understanding of the disease were being hampered by a narrow, specialized focus on its various symptoms.

Early Treatments

Starting in the 1950s, clinics specializing in the treatment of cystic fibrosis started to appear in the United States. At this same time, cystic fibrosis began to get attention as a widespread disease. Organizations were formed to promote research, raise money, and collect and publish information about it.

Although doctors had not learned what the cause of cystic fibrosis was, they made progress in treating it by attacking its symptoms. This progress was slow, and many mistakes were made. Not all treatments that were tried turned out to be effective. As time went on, however, cystic fibrosis patients began to live longer and more comfortable lives.

People with cystic fibrosis are prey to bacterial infections in their lungs. Doctors who prescribed antibiotics to treat these infections found that the treatments were more effective when cystic fibrosis was diagnosed early and the antibiotic therapy was started immediately. In the late 1970s, Danish physicians introduced a policy of giving regular, repeated three-month courses of antibiotics intravenously. That is, the doctors delivered the antibiotics directly into the bloodstream through a needle inserted into a vein. This treatment successfully fought some of the infections that afflict cystic fibrosis patients.

The excessive amounts of mucus that are present in the airways of patients with cystic fibrosis can prevent them from getting enough oxygen and can also lead to respiratory infections. In the 1960s, physicians in the United States began using a technique called mist tent therapy. Patients would sleep in a tent that was filled with a fine mist, the idea being that the mist would help improve their breathing by breaking up the mucus that blocked their airways. Many doctors and parents were convinced of the usefulness of this treatment, but studies eventually showed that mist tent therapy had few if any positive effects.

Since then, physicians have developed various techniques to drain mucus out of the airways. In a technique called postural drainage, patients are arranged in positions that encourage the fluid to drain from the airways, allowing the patients to spit the mucus out.

CGATTCTGAACATGATACGTACTGGTCCACTAGAACTGAACTCGAGAGGTACTAGA

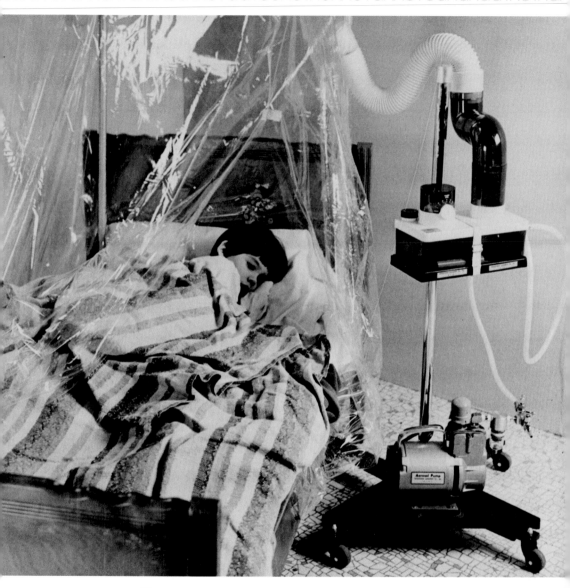

A young cystic fibrosis patient sleeps in a mist tent in this photo from 1970. The machine delivered moist, medicated air into the plastic tent to prevent the boy's lungs and airways from clogging. Many doctors felt the mist tents actually resulted in more infections and colds because the air became so damp. This treatment began to fall out of favor and was often replaced by nebulizers and aerosol inhalers.

Over the years, physicians scored an important success in treating the gastrointestinal symptoms of cystic fibrosis with special dietary supplements and pancreatic enzymes. It took many years of investigation—and trial and error—for doctors to figure out the best nutritional approach. For years, people with cystic fibrosis were advised to avoid fatty and high-protein foods because they are difficult for them to digest. However, later research showed that these foods are in fact important for the long-term survival of people with cystic fibrosis. Some important vitamins cannot be absorbed without fats. The amino acids in proteins help the body build cells, repair tissue, and form antibodies; carry oxygen throughout the body; and participate in muscle activity. Cystic fibrosis patients must eat more fat and protein than healthy people because their bodies are so inefficient at digesting and absorbing food and nutrients.

For many years, the supplemental pancreatic enzymes that patients were given were not very effective because most of them ended up being quickly destroyed by stomach acid. In the 1970s, however, researchers developed new pancreatic enzymes that could resist acid breakdown. After that, enzyme supplements helped patients with cystic fibrosis to consume and digest a wider variety of foods, which resulted in them being less vulnerable to malnutrition and vitamin deficiencies.

Identifying the Cystic Fibrosis Gene

The most significant advance in the history of cystic fibrosis research came in 1989, when scientists first identified the gene that, when defective, causes the disease. Scientists named this gene the cystic fibrosis transmembrane conductance regulator (CFTR). Scientists discovered that the job of

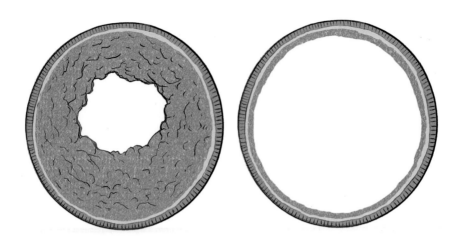

The thickened secretions (mucus) of a cystic fibrosis patient can block the airways of the lungs and windpipe. The graphic on the left depicts a blocked airway, while the image on the right represents a normal, healthy, open airway.

the protein produced by the CFTR gene is to regulate the normal flow of salt (sodium chloride) in and out of cells. Sodium chloride helps regulate safe body fluid levels and nerve impulses. The CFTR protein that is produced by the CFTR gene forms channels in cell membranes, especially in the cells lining the intestines and airways. These channels transport salt through the membranes. The salt is dissolved in water. When the salt passes through a cell membrane, so does the water in which it is dissolved (this process is known as osmosis).

When the CFTR gene is defective, the flow of salt and water in and out of cells is disrupted. Fluid regulation breaks down, resulting in many of the classic cystic fibrosis symptoms. Body fluids and secretions that are thin and slick in a healthy person—including saliva, mucus, sweat, and digestive juices—become thick and sticky in someone suffering

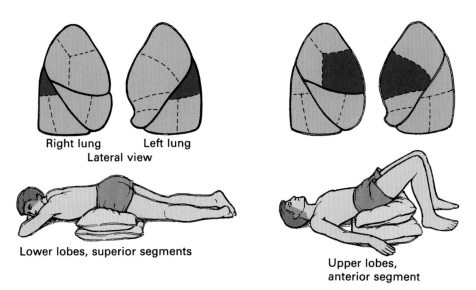

Right lung   Left lung
Lateral view

Lower lobes, superior segments

Upper lobes,
anterior segment

The above drawings show a cystic fibrosis patient in two different postural drainage positions. In the left-hand picture, the patient elevates his midsection while reclining on his stomach. This position helps drain mucus from the lower lobes on the outside edges of the lungs. The right-hand picture shows the patient on his back, with his hips and knees raised, helping to drain fluid from the upper lobes at the front of the lungs. Additional postural drainage positions help drain other areas of the lungs.

from cystic fibrosis. Mucus clogs the lungs, making breathing difficult and infections common. It can also block the duct in the liver where bile,which helps the body absorb fats, passes into the small intestine. The result can be permanent liver damage. The thickened digestive juices also clog the pancreas, preventing digestive enzymes produced there from making their way to the intestines where they can digest fats and proteins.

In addition to the role of sodium chloride in the cascade of symptoms associated with cystic fibrosis, some researchers believe that a similar imbalance of fatty acids may be an

CGATTCTGAACATGATACGTACTGGTCCACTAGAACTGAACTCGAGAGGTACTAG

important component of the disease. They have discovered that patients with cystic fibrosis have an unusually high level of one type of fatty acid and a deficiency of another. People who have a healthy CFTR gene have more evenly balanced levels of these fatty acids. It remains unclear what the effect of this imbalance is and exactly how it relates to the defective gene. There is hope, however, that by correcting these imbalances of fatty acids, the symptoms of cystic fibrosis may diminish or become more manageable.

While the discovery of the CFTR gene and defects to it helped paved the way for a better understanding of cystic fibrosis and the origins of its many debilitating symptoms, many mysteries surrounding the disease linger. Scientists hoped that the discovery of the CFTR gene would pave the way for better treatments—and perhaps even a cure—for cystic fibrosis. Almost two decades after the discovery of the CFTR gene, however, a cure for the disease remains frustratingly out of reach.

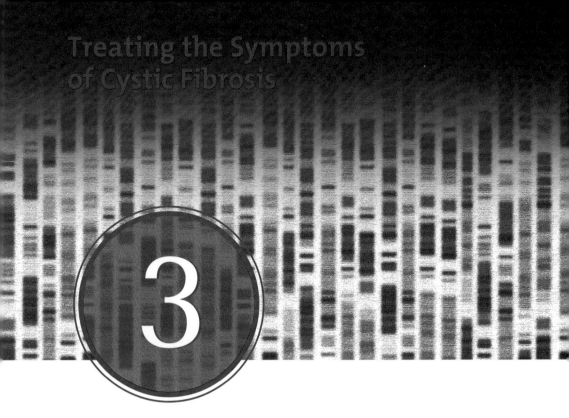

3

Cystic fibrosis used to be considered a childhood disease for the simple reason that most of the people who had it did not survive into adulthood. While a cure for the disease has not yet been found, people with cystic fibrosis are now living longer and healthier lives, thanks to greatly improved treatments. Today, 40 percent of people with cystic fibrosis are eighteen or older, with the average age of a person living with the disease being thirty-five. Some people with cystic fibrosis are surviving into their fifties and sixties. Today, most children with cystic fibrosis are well enough to attend school, and many adults work at part-time or full-time jobs.

CGATTCTGAACATGATACGTACTGGTCCACTAGAACTGAAGTGGAGAGGTACTAG

Nutrition and Cystic Fibrosis

Because cystic fibrosis hinders the body's ability to digest food and absorb nutrients from it, patients often suffer from malnutrition, low body weight, and a resulting decline in overall health. The digestive enzymes that become blocked in the pancreas and bile ducts and fail to reach the small intestine must be replaced by oral enzymes (enzymes in pill form that are swallowed). Babies with cystic fibrosis need to be given oral pancreatic enzymes to help them break down the starches, proteins, and fats found in milk and solid food. They also need to eat larger amounts of high-calorie food than other babies, since their digestive systems are much less efficient.

The thick secretions that block the pancreas in patients with cystic fibrosis prevent the digestion of fats and proteins and the absorption of the vitamins they contain, including vitamins A, D, E, and K. In order for people with cystic fibrosis to get these important nutrients, they must take daily vitamin supplements. They are also encouraged to consume vitamin-rich foods like fruits and vegetables and protein-rich foods like fish, eggs, and meat. Since maintaining a healthy weight is often difficult for those with cystic fibrosis, they are often put on high-fat, high-calorie diets that feature the kinds of food that health-conscious people generally try to eat sparingly, such as cheese, butter, chocolate, jam, pudding, bacon, and sausage.

Even with diets that are high in fat and calories, however, many people with cystic fibrosis fail to gain weight. They then require special nutritional supplements, in the form of milk shakes, fruit juices, or high-calorie powders and liquids. These help boost their intake of calories, fats, and proteins.

Sometimes, even these extra efforts to boost nutritional intake fail. Children with cystic fibrosis may fail to grow and

Hamburgers, hot dogs, french fries, onion rings, and greasy sandwiches constitute the kind of high-fat, high-protein, high-carbohydrate meal that doctors recommend for cystic fibrosis patients. Since their digestive systems are less efficient than those of healthy people, they have to eat especially rich, high-calorie foods in order to maintain a normal weight and avoid malnutrition.

develop properly. Adult sufferers experience significant weight loss, which often leaves physicians with no choice but to recommend tube feeding. Tubes attached to containers holding high-calorie, nutrient-enriched liquid food are inserted through a person's nose into the stomach or are inserted directly into the stomach. Since this tube feeding involves considerable discomfort for children, it is usually done when they are asleep.

ATCGATTCTGAACATGATACGTACTGGTCCACTAGAACTGAACTCGAGAGGTACTA

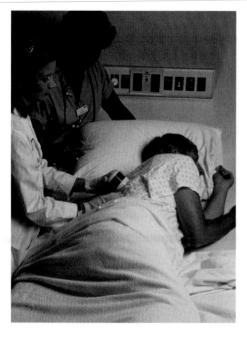

A cystic fibrosis patient receives a form of percussive therapy to help loosen mucus in the lungs. A nurse is holding an electronic device on the patient's back. The device emits vibrations that will help the patient cough up mucus.

Physiotherapy

Physiotherapy—a method of clearing the thick, sticky mucus from the lungs—is initiated upon diagnosis. Since it is necessary for patients to receive this form of treatment every day, physiotherapists teach parents how to give physiotherapy to their children themselves.

The most common form of physiotherapy for cystic fibrosis patients, known as percussive therapy, is performed manually by clapping the person on the back and on the chest area. The effect of this therapy is to loosen lung secretions and to stimulate coughing, both of which result in the expelling of mucus. It is recommended that percussive therapy be performed two times a day for twenty to thirty minutes. The patient should be lying on a bed with his or her head hanging over the edge. This position uses gravity to encourage the movement of mucus.

THE CYSTIC FIBROSIS FOUNDATION

In 1955, a group of physicians and parents who had children afflicted with cystic fibrosis established the Cystic Fibrosis Foundation (CFF). At the time, very little was known about the disease, and most affected children did not even live long enough to attend elementary school.

Since that time, the CFF has supported the development of over 115 cystic fibrosis care centers across the United States and has been a significant source of funding for the search for a cure and more effective treatments. The foundation provides grants to scientists to research the disease, and it supports a network of cystic fibrosis research centers at leading medical schools and universities across the United States.

The most important advance yet made in the treatment of the disease, the discovery of the gene whose malfunction is responsible for cystic fibrosis, was the result of research that was funded by the Cystic Fibrosis Foundation. The foundation has been responsible for funding research that has led to the development of important drugs for treating cystic fibrosis. The CFF has also been at the forefront of research efforts into the most promising of all the new treatments and possible cures—gene therapy.

CGATTCTGAACATGATACGTACTGGTCCACTAGAACTGAACTCGAGAGGTACTAG

By the age of two or three, children with cystic fibrosis are encouraged to participate in games that involve breathing exercises. By the time they get older, usually around the age of nine, this practice has prepared most children to be able to perform some physiotherapy for themselves. In addition, mechanical clappers and inflatable vibrating vests can perform the drainage. Older children and adults can use these on themselves without the assistance of a physiotherapist or family member.

Medication

Children and adults with cystic fibrosis need to take a variety of drugs to help fight the symptoms in their lungs and digestive tracts. Cystic fibrosis patients commonly take bronchodilator drugs, which open up the airways by relaxing the surrounding muscles and clearing away thick mucus secretions. This helps relieve tightness in a patient's airways and

This medical illustration depicts the passage of a bronchodilator drug through a constricted (tight and narrow) bronchiole of a lung. The drug widens the diameter of the bronchiole, allowing the patient to breathe more easily. The gray section is composed of mucus-secreting goblet cells. The red material is smooth muscle tissue that controls the airway's diameter.

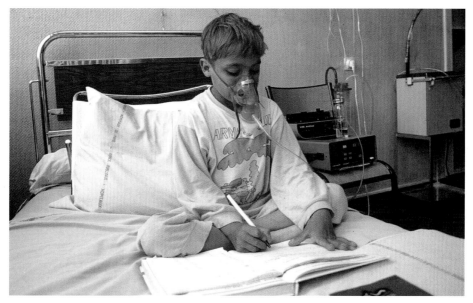

A young boy with cystic fibrosis breathes through a nebulizer in a hospital. A nebulizer is a device that delivers liquid medication in the form of a fine mist into a patient's airways. This treatment will loosen the mucus that builds up in the boy's airways due to the disease.

the resulting shortness of breath. In order to treat the chronic lung infections that afflict those with cystic fibrosis, antibiotics are usually prescribed. The antibiotics fight the bacteria that get trapped in the lungs by mucus. Inflammation of patients' airways can be treated with a certain kind of steroid. Steroids are hormones, or chemical signals, that regulate the body's growth and function. Corticosteroid hormones reduce inflammation (swelling) in part by adjusting the salt and water content of the body. Corticosteroids can be used to reduce the inflammation of the airways of patients with cystic fibrosis. In addition, mucus-thinning

ATCGATTCTGAACATGATACGTACTGGTCCACTAGAACTGAACTCGAGAGGTACTA

drugs may be taken to break up the clotted fluid and clear the airways.

Due to the chronic mineral deprivation that is typical of those living with cystic fibrosis, adult patients sometimes develop osteoporosis, a condition caused by calcium loss that is characterized by thinning and brittle bones. Drugs called bisphosphonates, which are used to treat osteoporosis in older women, are also beneficial for the treatment of osteoporosis in people with cystic fibrosis. Because the pancreas—where insulin-producing cells are found—and bile ducts of the liver are attacked by cystic fibrosis, patients often eventually develop diabetes and serious, potentially fatal liver problems. The same medications that are used to treat these conditions in other people are also used to treat people with cystic fibrosis.

4

In 1989, when genetic researchers succeeded in isolating the cystic fibrosis gene, everyone hoped that dramatic improvements in the treatment of the disease were just around the corner. Unfortunately, such breakthroughs have been slow in coming. Scientists still find themselves pursuing many different avenues of research and developing many different approaches for improving the health of people with cystic fibrosis. No single, simple solution to the disease has yet been found.

Screening for the Cystic Fibrosis Gene

Eventually, the discovery of the cystic fibrosis gene may lead to a cure for the disease by

ATCGATTCTGAACATGATACGTACTGGTCCACTAGAAGTGAACTCGAGAGGTACTA

allowing doctors to correct the defective gene or insert a properly working CFTR protein directly into cells. However, the immediate benefit of the discovery of the CFTR gene is that it is now possible to screen couples hoping to become parents and unborn children for the genetic defect.

Parents can be tested to find out if they are carriers. A simple laboratory test of blood or saliva will reveal whether or not their CFTR genes are defective. Test results are not always accurate, however. The tests cannot detect all of the different mutations of the CFTR gene. In rare cases, persons whose test results are normal nevertheless turn out to be carriers.

The so-called sweat test remains the standard means of diagnosing cystic fibrosis. These days, the test is administered by applying a sweat-producing chemical on a small patch of skin on the leg or arm. An electrode is then attached to that area. The painless and hardly noticeable electrical current that passes through the electrode stimulates the skin and sweat glands. The resulting perspiration is collected and sent to a lab, which measures the salt content of the sweat. The test has to be given twice because inaccurate results occasionally occur. Sometimes the test indicates that someone has cystic fibrosis when they really do not (a "false positive"). Other times the result is a "false negative," incorrectly indicating that someone does not have the disease when, in fact, they do. The test also cannot indicate how severe a form of the disease a person has, nor can it be given to babies younger than one month old. Newborns often do not produce enough sweat to be tested.

There are two tests that have been developed to detect the presence of cystic fibrosis in a fetus. They both involve extracting placenta or fluid from the mother's womb. One prenatal test for cystic fibrosis is chorionic villus sampling (CVS). In CVS, a tiny piece of the placenta is removed for laboratory inspection in order to detect whether or not the DNA in the tissue sample

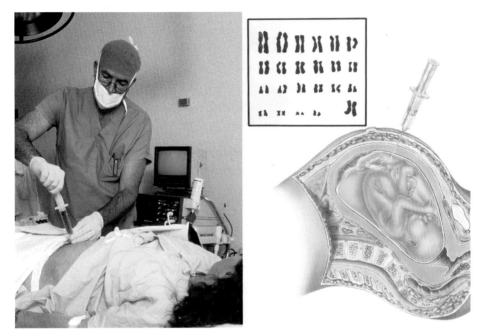

Amniocentesis is a procedure in which a sample of amniotic fluid (the liquid that fills the womb) is removed. The fluid contains fetal cells whose DNA can be tested to detect any abnormalities in the fetus's chromosomes that may indicate birth defects or inherited diseases. A diagram of the procedure appears at right, while a doctor is shown performing an amniocentesis at left. The graphic at top right is a chart of normal female chromosomes.

contains the defective CFTR gene. The other test that is used to detect the presence of the defective CFTR gene in the fetus is amniocentesis. This involves extracting a sample of the amniotic fluid surrounding the baby and testing it to see whether the fetal cells present in it contain the defective CFTR gene.

Both tests are what doctors call invasive, and in rare cases they pose a danger to the fetus. In addition, developing fetuses cannot be treated for or cured of cystic fibrosis, so a diagnosis serves mainly to prepare the parents for what may lie ahead.

New Treatments for Cystic Fibrosis

Many new treatments for cystic fibrosis are being developed by researchers working for universities, drug companies, and genetic engineering firms around the world.

A Device to Clear Mucus from Airways

One new treatment for clearing mucus from the airways of cystic fibrosis sufferers involves the use of a device called a flutter. A flutter looks and works like a pipe. A person exhales through it, triggering a special valve in the flutter that creates rapid air pressure fluctuations in the person's airways. The vibrations have the effect of loosening mucus from the airways. In one study, the flutter was found to be three times more effective in clearing mucus than conventional percussive therapy. Only time will tell whether the use of the flutter device will help delay or prevent long-term lung damage in patients with cystic fibrosis.

Aerosol Antibiotics

Antibiotics—a powerful class of drugs that have the ability to kill bacteria, enabling people to recover quickly from infections—are used to treat the bacterial lung infections that often occur with cystic fibrosis. Researchers are currently trying to develop a new class of antibiotics designed to kill the specific bacteria that infect the lungs of cystic fibrosis sufferers.

Until recently, antibiotics had to be administered intravenously in order to be effective in patients with the disease. The new antibiotic therapies that have been developed to fight cystic fibrosis–specific infections are administered in aerosol form (a pressurized mist). Inhaling the drug enables it to attack the infected lung tissues directly, making the drug more powerful and effective. Administering antibiotics in this more efficient, targeted way has the additional advantage

New technology, like this aerosol inhaler, enables liquid medication to be inhaled through the lungs with greater efficiency, maximizing the amount of medication that actually reaches the airways. Greater efficiency of medication delivery allows patients to use smaller amounts of medication, resulting in fewer side effects and lower costs.

of reducing the amount of drug that is needed per dose. This reduces the risk of patients experiencing dangerous side effects from the antibiotics, such as hearing loss and kidney problems.

Targeted Treatments for Specific Mutations

Cystic fibrosis is the result of any one of hundreds of different mutations of the CFTR gene. All these mutations of the CFTR gene interfere with its proper functioning in only slightly different ways. The variations in severity of the disease can be attributed to these differences in mutations.

ATCGATTCTGAACATGATACGTACTGGTCCACTAGAACTGAAGTCGGAGAGGTACTA

The focus of some cystic fibrosis research is on distinguishing between the different CFTR gene mutations and identifying their specific effects. Some researchers are exploring the possibility of developing targeted therapies that take these different mutations into account. For example, the effect of one mutation, called the delta F508 mutation, is that the CFTR protein degrades (breaks down) before it reaches the cell membrane. Once degraded, it cannot begin its assigned job of providing channels in the membrane through which sodium chloride and water can pass. As a result, the cells cannot transport salt, and the regulation of water content breaks down.

In experiments that involved keeping the cells at temperatures below what human beings can tolerate, scientists were able to get the deformed proteins produced by the delta F508 mutation to remain stable enough to successfully perform the normal function of an undamaged CFTR protein. While a therapy that depends on subjecting the body to uncomfortably or even dangerously low temperatures is not practical, this discovery nevertheless points the way toward a viable future research goal—treating cases of cystic fibrosis that result from the delta F508 mutation by helping the protein get to the cell membrane before it disintegrates.

Blocking Excessive Sodium Absorption

As previously discussed, in normal cells, the CFTR gene controls and balances the absorption of sodium by allowing water to pass through the cell membranes. One consequence of a malfunctioning CFTR gene is the interruption of the flow of water out of the body's cells, especially the cells of the respiratory system. The flow of water is affected by a disruption in the normal balance of sodium chloride levels in airway cells. A healthy CFTR gene will create a channel in cell membranes that transports chloride ions out of the cells. It also helps regulate similar sodium channels.

When cells are governed by a defective CFTR gene, the cells decrease their secretions of chloride while increasing their absorption of sodium. The flow of water is affected by these disruptions in salt levels, resulting in greater absorption of water by cells. This means that mucus and other airway secretions have less water in them than usual, since airway cells are absorbing more than the usual amount of water. The result is the thick, sticky mucus that is present in the bronchial tubes and the pancreatic ducts of people with cystic fibrosis. Ordinarily these systems are lubricated by thin, slick, watery secretions. One of the goals of current cystic fibrosis research is to develop safe and effective drugs that can prevent this increase in sodium absorption in cells lining the airways.

5

The ultimate hope for finding a cure for cystic
fibrosis lies in gene therapy, a new field that
has the potential to reprogram malfunctioning
cells. Gene therapy involves the insertion of
normal or genetically altered genes into cells
that possess malfunctioning genes. Inserting
these healthy genes gives the cells new instruc-
tions. In essence, they reprogram the cells to
work properly.

   In the case of cystic fibrosis, scientists
have found that inserting a normal CFTR gene
into a cell that has an abnormal CFTR gene
allows that cell to begin producing a properly
functioning CFTR protein. Since the root
cause of cystic fibrosis appears to be the
malfunction of the CFTR gene, scientists
believe that inserting copies of the properly

Gunter Blobel stands in his lab at the Howard Hughes Medical Institute in New York City. In 1999, Dr. Blobel was awarded the Nobel Prize for Medicine for his discovery that proteins have signals that guide their movement in the cell. This discovery may be used to help treat cystic fibrosis. The cystic fibrosis protein does not move to the correct "address" in the cell. If its signal can be fixed, the protein could travel to the appropriate part of the cell and begin to function properly.

working gene into cells of the affected organs and tissues will one day provide a cure.

Vectors

Genes are so small that they cannot be seen even under a microscope. Therefore, inserting them into cells presents scientists with something of a challenge. One effective method of gene therapy involves the use of biological tools called vectors. A vector is something that has the ability to guide or transport. Viruses are very useful biological vectors.

The reason scientists decided to try using viruses to transport genes into cells has to do with the way viruses function. Viruses are not able to reproduce on their own. The only way they can reproduce is by inserting themselves into the cells of other creatures, in effect taking over the cells' machinery in order to produce copies of themselves. So, in order to replicate, viruses are programmed to move into host cells and alter the host cells' makeup. This makes viruses an excellent vehicle with which to deliver healthy genes to a cell in need of genetic repair.

One complication is that viruses are not benign, or harmless, organisms. Since viruses are germs that very efficiently spread disease—diseases that range in severity from the common cold to AIDS—scientists have had to figure out how to trick viruses into transporting good genes into cells without also causing disease. Scientists used restriction enzymes—the same tools cells use to manipulate genes and proteins—to cut genes from DNA strands and splice them into the genetic material of the viruses. Restriction enzymes are also used to remove genes from viruses. This prevents them from performing some of their functions. If the right genes are cut from them, the viruses become harmless. By modifying the viruses, scientists have succeeded in getting them to transport healthy CFTR genes into malfunctioning cells. One class of the viruses that has been used most extensively for this kind of gene therapy is adenoviruses, which cause about 10 percent of all acute respiratory infections in children.

In experiments conducted in 1990, scientists successfully used a modified adenovirus to deposit normal genes directly into airway cells damaged by cystic fibrosis. This "correction" of the cells occurred in a petri dish, not in an actual human subject.

Dr. Ronald Crystal of the National Heart, Lung, and Blood Institute in Bethesda, Maryland, is working on a nasal spray made of genetically engineered protein that breaks up the infected lung-clogging mucus of cystic fibrosis patients. Such a treatment significantly improves both the ease and efficiency of their breathing.

In October 1993, scientists at the University of Iowa achieved a major victory in cystic fibrosis gene therapy by successfully repairing the defective airway cells of patients with the use of vectors. This achievement gave researchers hope that gene therapy could work, but it was far from being a cure for cystic fibrosis. The benefits of the trial were small, with the respiratory health of the patients improving only slightly and only for a short time. A 2002 trial, however, led to significant improvement in lung function after gene transfer,

ATCGATTCTGAACATGATACGTACTGGTCCACTAGAACTGAACTCGAGAGGTACTAC

the first time ever that prolonged improvement was observed after gene therapy.

Some researchers are now experimenting with the use of retroviruses—the class of viruses that includes HIV, the virus that causes AIDS. Researchers are modifying retroviruses (using restriction enzymes) in such a way that they can be safely used for gene therapy. After inactivating the HIV virus, scientists were able to use it as a vector to deliver healthy CFTR genes in cystic fibrosis cells. In some cases, researchers remove the genes that enable the virus to reproduce. Other times, they remove the genes that the virus uses to cause particular disease symptoms.

Nonviral Vectors and Plasmids

Other areas of research that are currently being explored include investigating how nonviral vectors called liposomes can be used to transfer genes to cells. Liposomes are fatty substances that naturally adhere to the surfaces of cells. Coating the gene with liposomes protects it and facilitates entry into the cell, where it can begin to repair the damage caused by the malfunctioning cystic fibrosis gene.

Still other researchers are developing a technology known as PLASmin, which involves compressing individual molecules of DNA down to their minimum size. Decreasing the size of these molecules makes it easier for scientists to introduce the new compressed gene into the cell, without having to use a virus or other kind of biological vector to carry it. The DNA is delivered directly to airway cells via nose drops, a broncho-scope (flexible tube that extends down the windpipe), or an aerosol inhaler, and to other tissues through the bloodstream.

In all of these various trials, scientists have been focusing on treating the airway cells of patients with cystic fibrosis. There are two reasons for this. First, those are the easiest of all cystic fibrosis–affected cells to reach. Second, the lung damage associated with cystic fibrosis is the most life-threatening complication of the disease. Ultimately, researchers hope to apply the same techniques of gene therapy to the other organs affected by the disease, especially the pancreas. By eventually targeting all of the cells of the organs and systems damaged by cystic fibrosis, doctors will make progress in treating the many digestive, respiratory, circulatory, and reproductive disorders that have confused medical science for hundreds of years.

Obstacles to Gene Therapy

The early successes that immediately followed the discovery of the cystic fibrosis gene convinced scientists that gene therapy had the potential to ultimately cure the disease, or at least be a highly effective treatment for it. The progress that scientists have made so far with gene therapy has convinced them they are on the right track.

Still, there are many obstacles that remain to be overcome. For one thing, the body regards all viruses as invaders, even those that are rendered inactive and contain beneficial genes. The immediate response of the immune system is to attack them, as it would any virus. Many of these vectors are attacked and destroyed before they can deliver the healthy gene to a diseased cell, and the immune system often produces symptoms of illness. This is one reason researchers are experimenting with nonviral vectors.

Another problem with gene therapy is that while genes might do the work scientists intend them to do after they are inserted in the cells, they do so only temporarily. For some reason, in all experiments that have been conducted so far, the inserted gene eventually stopped working. While these

CGATTCTGAACATGATACGTACTGGTCGAGTAGAACTGAACTCGAGAGGTACTAGA

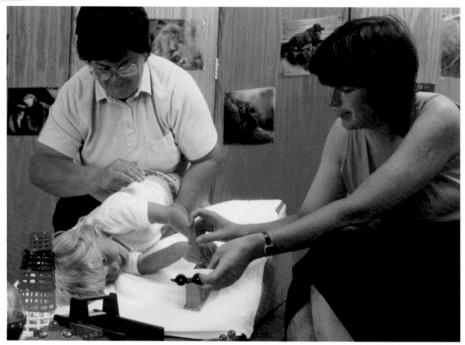

A young cystic fibrosis patient receives care and treatment from a medical professional. At this point in time, this child can be expected to live into adulthood. With new research and treatments, it is hoped that she will be able to be cured some day.

gene therapies have been successful in improving the functioning of the airways of people with cystic fibrosis, their positive and life-sustaining effects have, unfortunately, been only temporary.

Despite the halting and tentative progress of these trials, gene therapy still represents the brightest hope for treating the many debilitating symptoms of cystic fibrosis and, most important, curing the disease. Modern medical science has already made great strides in extending the lives and increasing the health of people with cystic fibrosis. The work being done right now in labs around the world may soon allow them to live entirely normal, healthy lives.

Timeline

1938

Dr. Dorothy Andersen of Columbia-Presbyterian's Babies and Children's Hospital is the first to describe the symptoms of the disease and names it "cystic fibrosis of the pancreas."

1953

Dr. Paul di Sant'Agnese, also of Babies and Children's Hospital, develops the sweat test (which measures the chloride content in sweat) to diagnose cystic fibrosis. It remains the standard diagnostic tool used today.

1955

The Cystic Fibrosis Foundation is formed by a group of doctors, parents of young patients, and volunteers. Average life expectancy for cystic fibrosis patients is five years.

1966

The Cystic Fibrosis Foundation creates a patient data registry, which tracks the case histories of patients being treated at foundation care centers.

1978

The first nationwide fund-raising event, "Bowl for Breath," is held and doubles the fund-raising dollars for cystic fibrosis.

(continued on following page)

(continued from previous page)

1982

The Cystic Fibrosis Foundation creates the Research Development Program (RDP) to encourage cutting-edge research into the causes of the disease, as well as treatments and a possible cure.

1983

Research demonstrates that the cells lining the lungs of cystic fibrosis sufferers do not move chloride into the airways properly.

1985

Life expectancy reaches twenty-five years.

1989

Doctors Francis Collins, John Riordan, and Lap-Chee Tsui discover the gene responsible for cystic fibrosis.

1993

Pulmozyme, a drug that breaks down thick mucus, is approved for use by cystic fibrosis patients by the Food and Drug Administration (FDA). The first gene therapy trial using human testing demonstrates that the therapy can correct malfunctioning nasal cells affected by the cystic fibrosis gene.

2002

Clinical trials show that the drug azithromycin helps improve lung function in cystic fibrosis patients.

2003

With the support of the Cystic Fibrosis Foundation, a company called Targeted Genetics, Inc., begins the largest and most advanced gene therapy trial to date for cystic fibrosis.

2004

Almost two dozen treatments for the disease are in development. Life expectancy is now in the mid-thirties for people with cystic fibrosis.

amniotic fluid The fluid in which an embryo or fetus is suspended in the womb.

carrier Someone who bears or transmits the agent that causes or triggers a disease but does not suffer from the disease him- or herself.

cell The smallest structural unit of living matter that is capable of functioning independently and performing the basic functions of life (such as motion, digestion, and reproduction).

chorionic villus sampling A diagnostic procedure in which fetal cells are obtained from the placenta tissue of a pregnant woman. The cells' DNA is tested for the presence of defective CFTR genes.

chromosome A DNA-containing structure in the nucleus of a cell.

clinic A facility (sometimes within a hospital) for the diagnosis and treatment of patients not staying at the hospital overnight.

diagnosis The act of identifying a disease based on the evidence of a patient's symptoms.

DNA Deoxyribonucleic acid; the long, double-stranded molecule that is the basis of human heredity.

electrolyte A nonmetallic substance that, when dissolved in a suitable solvent, becomes a conductor, or carrier, of electric charges. These electrical charges allow the body's muscles and nerves to work properly.

enzymes Proteins produced by the body that cause specific biochemical reactions to take place.

fetus A developing vertebrate. In humans, the bundle of cells that result from conception is called an embryo. After three months, it is referred to as a fetus.

gastrointestinal Relating to the stomach and intestine.

gene The basic unit of inheritance, by which traits such as hair and eye color, height, and other physical characteristics are passed on to offspring.

genetic disorder A disease linked to malfunctions in the process of biological inheritance.

glucose A kind of sugar.

membrane A soft, pliable sheet or layer.

metabolize To process substances produced in a living body.

mucus A thick, slippery secretion that protects the membranes where it is produced.

mutation A permanent change in the hereditary material, usually caused by a change in the chemical makeup of a gene.

pancreas A large gland in vertebrates that produces and releases digestive enzymes and the hormones insulin and glucagon.

protein One of a large group of extremely complex, naturally organic molecules consisting of linked amino acids. They contain the elements carbon, hydrogen, nitrogen, oxygen, usually sulphur, and occasionally other elements. Proteins perform a great variety of important jobs in the body, including building and repairing cells.

respiratory Related to breathing, the physical and chemical processes by which an organism supplies its tissues with oxygen.

solute A substance that is dissolved in a solvent, thus forming a solution.

virus A submicroscopic infectious agent that is capable of growth and multiplication only inside living cells.

For More Information

The Boomer Esiason Foundation
417 Fifth Avenue, Second Floor
New York, NY 10016
(646) 344-3765
Web site: http://www.esiason.org

Canadian Cystic Fibrosis Foundation
2221 Yonge Street, Suite 601
Toronto, ON M4S 2B4
Canada
(416) 485-9149
Web site: http://www.ccff.ca

Cystic Fibrosis Foundation
6931 Arlington Road
Bethesda, MD 20814
(301) 951-4422
(800) FIGHT CF (344-4823)
Web site: http://www.cff.org/

Cystic Fibrosis Research, Inc.
2672 Bayshore Parkway, Suite 520
Mountain View, CA 94043

(650) 404-9975
Web site: http://www.cfri.org/home.htm

March of Dimes
1275 Mamaroneck Avenue
White Plains, NY 10605
Web site: http://www.marchofdimes.com

Web Sites
Due to the changing nature of Internet links, the Rosen
Publishing Group, Inc., has developed an online list of Web
sites related to the subject of this book. This site is updated
regularly. Please use this link to access the list:

http://www.rosenlinks.com/gdd/cyfi

For Further Reading

Abramovitz, Melissa. *Cystic Fibrosis*. San Diego, CA: Lucent Books, 2003.

Anderson, Peggy. *Children's Hospital*. New York, NY: Harper & Row, 1985.

Gold, Susan D. *Cystic Fibrosis*. Mankato, MN: Crestwood House, 2000.

Gray, Susan Heinrichs. *Living with Cystic Fibrosis* (Living Well Chronic Conditions). Chanhassen, MN: Child's World, 2002.

Kepron, Wayne. *Cystic Fibrosis: Everything You Need to Know* (Your Personal Health). Richmond Hill, ON, Canada: Firefly Books, 2004.

Klane, Roger. *Gregor Mendel: Father of Genetics*. Berkeley Heights, NJ: Enslow, 1997.

Krasnow, David. *Genetics*. Milwaukee, WI: Gareth Stevens Publishing, 2003.

Lee, Justin, *Everything You Need to Know About Cystic Fibrosis*. New York, NY: Rosen Publishing Group, 2001.

Lipman, Andy. *Alive at 25: How I'm Beating Cystic Fibrosis* (Understanding Health and Sickness). Athens, GA: Longstreet Press, 2002.

Monroe, Judy. *Cystic Fibrosis.* Mankato, MN: Capstone Press, 2001.

Snedden, Robert. *Cell Division and Genetics.* Portsmouth, NH: Heinemann, 2002.

Wilcox, Fred H. *DNA: The Thread of Life.* Minneapolis, MN: Lerner, 1988.

Bibliography

Cystic Fibrosis Foundation. "About Cystic Fibrosis." May
  2005. Retrieved October 2005 (http://www.cff.org/
  about_cf/what_is_cf/).
Doershuk, Carl F. *Cystic Fibrosis in the Twentieth Century:
  People, Events, and Progress.* Cleveland, OH: AM
  Publishing, 2002.
Harris, Ann, and Maurice Super. *Cystic Fibrosis: The Facts.*
  New York, NY: Oxford University Press, 1995.
Hawley, R. Scott, and Catherine A. Mori. *The Human
  Genome: A User's Guide.* San Diego, CA: Academic Press,
  1999.
Hopkin, Karen. *Understanding Cystic Fibrosis* (Understanding
  Health and Sickness). Jackson, MS: University Press of
  Mississippi, 1998.
Mayo Clinic. "Diseases and Conditions: Cystic Fibrosis."
  March 2005. Retrieved October 2005 (http://
  www.mayoclinic.com/health/cystic-fibrosis/DS00287).
Orenstein, David M. *Cystic Fibrosis: A Guide for Patient and
  Family.* 3rd ed. Philadelphia, PA: Lippincott Williams &
  Wilkins, 2003.
Orenstein, David M., Beryl J. Rosenstein, and Robert C. Stern.
  Cystic Fibrosis: Medical Care. Philadelphia, PA: Lippincott
  Williams & Wilkins, 2000.

Shapiro, Robert. *The Human Blueprint: The Race to Unlock the Secrets of Our Genetic Script.* New York, NY: St. Martin's Press, 1991.

U.S. Congress Office of Technology Assessment. *Cystic Fibrosis and DNA Tests: Implications of Carrier Screening.* Washington, DC: U.S. Government Printing Office, 1992. OTA-A-532.

Yankaskas, James R., and Michael R. Knowles, eds. *Cystic Fibrosis in Adults.* Philadelphia, PA: Lippincott Williams & Wilkins, 1999.

Index

About the Author

Maxine Rosaler is a writer who specializes in medical subjects. She has written books on various diseases and disorders, including measles, botulism, listeriosis, and Asperger's syndrome. She lives and works in New York City.

Photo Credits

Designer: Evelyn Horovicz